T0253261

LOU

Breanna Carzoo

HARPER
An Imprint of HarperCollinsPublishers

Lou

Copyright © 2022 by Breanna Carzoo

All rights reserved. Manufactured in Italy.

No part of this book may be used or reproduced in any manner
whatsoever without written permission except in the case of
brief quotations embodied in critical articles and reviews. For
information address HarperCollins Children's Books, a division of
HarperCollins Publishers, 195 Broadway, New York, NY 10007.
www.harpercollinschildrens.com

ISBN 978-0-06-305405-9

23 24 25 26 RTLO 10 9 8 7 6 5 4

❖

First Edition

To Chris, for seeing greatness in me
before I saw it in myself

Hello!

Can you see me down here?

My name is Lou, and I'm...

a toilet.

All day,

every day,

one by one...

they SNIFF

and TWIRL

and **TWIST**

and **LIFT**

and...

well, you know.

I know I'm useful.

It's just that sometimes...

deep down inside,

I feel like there's more in me than what they can see.

Like I'm full of greatness!

I just don't know what it is

or how to let it out.

And can I tell you something?
Just between you and me?

I worry sometimes.

What if this is all I am? All I'll ever be?

What if I never do anything more...

...important?

Oh no, here we go again.

One by one, they...

SNIFF and

Uh, do I see smoke?

TWIRL and

Wait! What's going on?

TWIST and

Whoa, that feels really weird.

LIFT!

Ah! Why's everyone looking at me?

Oh! I see it now!
I know what I have to do!

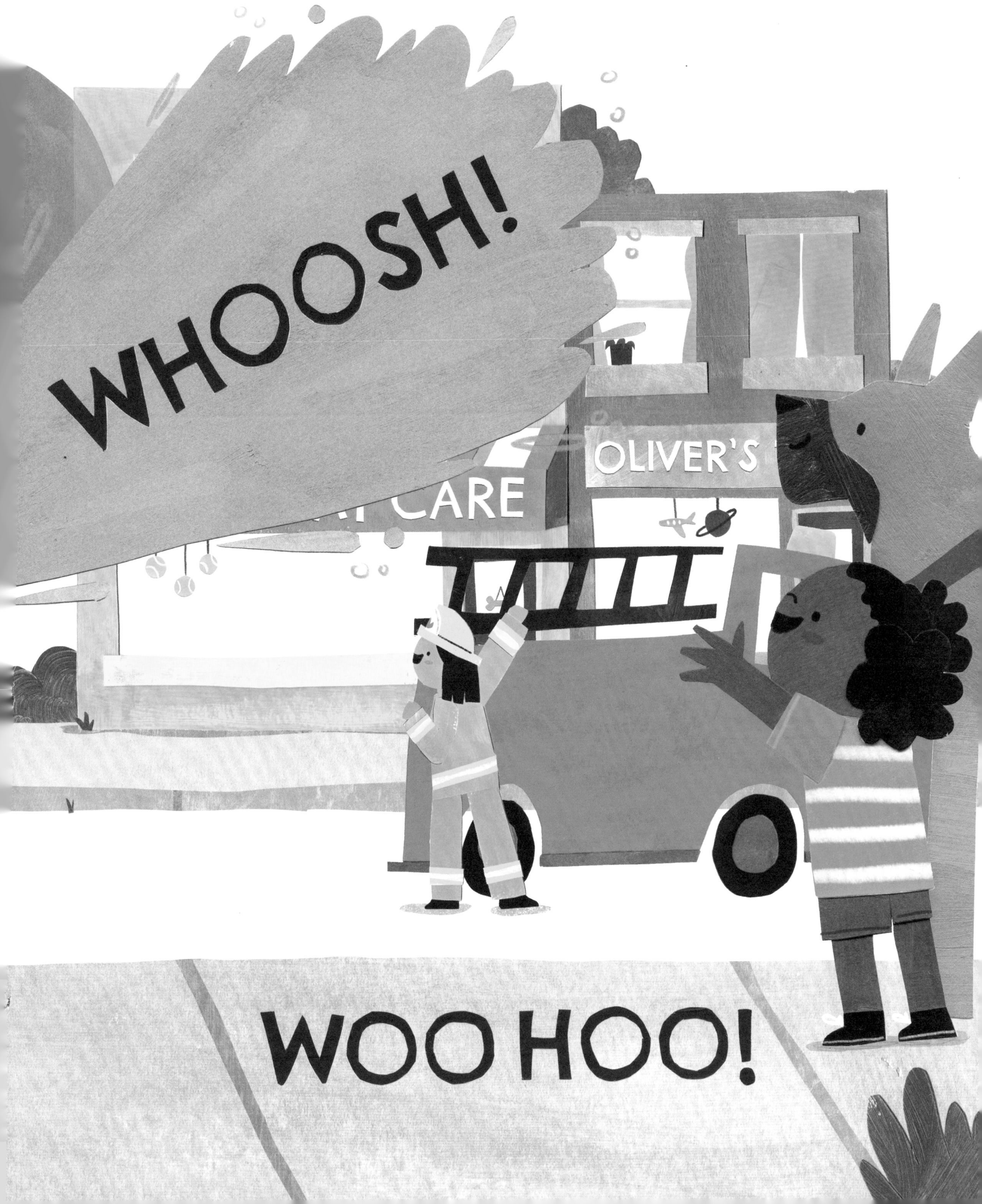
WHOOSH!
OLIVER'S
CARE
WOO HOO!

How did I not see this before?
My name is Lou, and I'm...

a superhero!